THE GLOBAL ADVENTURES OF
ARGUILLE MacGREGOR

ARGUILLE MacGREGOR

Word Art Publishing
9350 Wilshire Blvd
Suite 203, Beverly Hills, CA 90212
www.wordartpublishing.com
Phone: 1 (888) 614 - 1370

Published by Word Art Publishing

ISBN: Paperback   978-1-955070-42-3
        Hardback   978-1-955070-44-7
        Ebook   978-1-955070-43-0

PREFACE

THE SERIES OF short stories that follow are inspired by people from all walks of life. The timelines vary, but the locations are accurate. The characters names are fictitious, but their roles are also adapted from life stories. This series of short stories involves the adventures of Arguille Macgregor as he travels the globe. Arguille's sense of adventure to travel to these many locations and to experience the different cultures is caused by his interest in his Scottish/Irish heritage and by having multicultural parents.

The Kidnap Attempt

SOUTH AMERICA HAD always intrigued Arguille and had stirred his curiosity when broaching the subject in conversations with his engineering friends. Acquaintances who had traveled to the various countries recanted tales of political intrigue, danger, gorgeous *chica*s, international cuisine, and a beautiful countryside. When a professional friend invited him to make a short-term visit to Colombia and to lend his expertise to the design and construction quality of a totally integrated mine facility in the remote Colombian jungle, he accepted his invitation during the same conversation.

His visit to Colombia would require frequent trips to operations and the port vessel loading operations from his living quarters, which would be in Caesar and Santa Marta respectively. As the operations expanded, many new infrastructures and facility projects would have to be designed, erected, and commissioned to international standards, which would be the direct responsibility of Arguille.

The port had received its total mine production from the 120-kilometer (75-mile) rail line, had stored the material, and had put it on one-hundred-thousand-ton Panamax ocean vessels for transport to various international customers. Panamax vessels met the dimensional limits of the Panama Canal. All rail traffic went through guerilla-active areas from mine to port.

An expatriate staff was maintained for administration and supervision. Because the facility operated on a 24-7 schedule, it required dining facilities for all workers and living quarters for the expats. The expats' living quarters included a safe room with eighteen-inch-thick reinforced concrete walls and massive steel doors. The safe room was for the security of expats in the event of an attack by guerrilla forces. The guerrilla forces were members of the FARC (Revolutionary Armed Forces of Colombia). FARC was a communist left-wing military organization that supported itself f inancially through drug sales and k idnapping-ransom dollars.

Port operations were situated on the Caribbean's coastline (latitude ten degrees), which gave it a tropical climate with palm trees, sandy beaches, iguanas, ocean breezes, and mosquitoes. Because the three types of climate varied from hot, wet, to hotter, many indigenous varieties of cacti were prolific in the severe dry seasons of November through January.

The supervisors worked a two-week-on-one-week-off basis. They traveled by private jets on Saturdays from the US to Cartagena and then on to the operation near Cesar or Santa Marta near the port. Two weeks later, they returned to the US, reversing the route.

Traveling by car between operations was prohibited due to the potential of robbery and kidnapping. When travel by vehicle was an absolute necessity, two armed guards plus an armored vehicle with two additional armed guards escorted them.

A one-week R & R was allowed between each two-week work trip. As the working hours were 24/7 on call, this was an accommodating break.

Arguille traveled to mine operations and port sites on one of the available King Air planes, which was a single-engine Cessna, or by boat—the Santa Marta Airport was only accessible by sea. The

Cessna required fifteen additional minutes to make the port trip from Cartagena, unlike the King Air craft. One thing that he noticed while at the Santa Marta boat access was one of Pablo Escobar's mansions. Pablo had the distinction of being the Colombian drug Czar of the Medellin drug cartel.

The president of the company was one of the passengers on an arriving flight from the US. As often was the case, he would make unannounced visits to operations. He was a very intelligent leader who had taken Colombian operations from its infancy to its success during an eleven-year period. He orchestrated all aspects: designs, commercial contracts, labor agreements, and infrastructure development. He was a dynamic individual who commanded the respect of his subordinates.

One event he had scheduled for this visit was a trip to the port. The most convenient time for this travel occurred on the following Saturday. Operations arranged to have one of the Cessnas available for his transportation to port operations. As Arguille had construction issues to address there, he had also requested to tag along to cover his needs. The flight time from Cartagena was one hour and fifteen minutes on the Cessna. We also had to travel twenty minutes by road from the airport to port operations.

During my time in Colombia, guerilla activity was sporadic but active with rail interruptions and highway attacks. All were attempts to kidnap wealthy visitors and businesspeople and to marshal them into the Sierra Nevada de Santa Marta for concealment. From there, messages would be delivered to owners or family members demanding ransoms.

The left-leaning FARC (Revolutionary Armed Force of Colombia) had been perpetuating highway robberies and attacks in local businesses. The kidnapping of wealthy Colombians and expats were regular occurrences. On some occasions, the bandits would block highways, forcing vehicles with families to stop. Any jewelry or cash was taken at gunpoint. Then the hostages were moved to a remote, dense jungle location. After being captured with his family, one individual had been told to return with money while the rest of the family had been held hostage. If no money had been brought, the remaining family members would have been murdered.

Rail access between the mine and the port covered 125 kilometers (78 miles) through marshlands, villages, and jungles. Thirty-five elevated bridges and trestles along the route created ample weak links where traffic could easily be stopped. This was attempted on a weekly basis. Explosives would be placed under the tracks and would be detonated when the unit's train approached. Colombian transportation laws required that lone workers must ride in the last car of the unit's train. In the event that any guerillas attacked the last half of the train, supervisors and security could be notified. Any employees who remained with the train after the explosives were detonated would be kidnapped for a ransom.

The morning Arguille was to travel to the port, he awoke at 5:00 a.m. in his eighth-floor Cartagena apartment with its kitchenette. The morning's eastern sunrise was a rude awakening but was also effective. While consuming Colombian coffee on his balcony that faced the ocean, Arguille could observe local women with aluminum pans of freshly caught sea bass and snappers walking the streets and advertised *piscados* for sale. Subsequently, fresh pan-fried fish and eggs over easy were a breakfast standard.

At 6:00 a.m., an armed escort, along with the company president, arrived at the apartment to pick him up for the short trip to the airport. They all assumed that the Cessna would be there transport, but due to a mechanical issue, they changed to the King Air plane, which would make the trip in fifteen minutes less time. Little did they understand the magnitude of the effect this mechanical event would have on there short-term future.

A company of armed security personnel with an armored vehicle greeted them. They proceeded onto a two-lane asphalt highway, crossed over a single-lane bridge, and moved on to the port's security check-in point. The entire journey from the airport to the operation's site only took twenty minutes.

After check-in at the operational office. Arguille proceeded to his office, which was in the brick-and-mortar, single-story administration building. He had not been at his desk more than five minutes when the lead security guard entered his office and told him that he needed to go immediately to the safe room. All expats and secretaries were also sent to the room for their protection because they were under attack.

The guard had informed them the guerillas had blocked the only single-lane bridge, which they had just crossed. The FARC guerillas had been trying to capture the company's president.

They proceeded en masse to the safe room. The steel entrance was secured once they were inside.

They later learned that the guerillas had obtained the company president's traveling schedule and had planned to block the van at the single-lane bridge. Earlier in the month, He had also observed an ultralight aircraft occasionally flying over the facility. Overhead photos of the port facility were later found when company security had raided a guerilla staging area near the port. Port security had not realized that the pilot had been on a recon mission for the guerillas and had been capturing the port's infrastructure in aerial photos.

The photos had given the guerillas valuable information. From the information obtained by the team, they found the guerillas were not only going to capture the company's president at the single-lane bridge while our vehicle was stopped but also all expats from the administration building. Then they would make a dash for the thick jungle's undergrowth, which was near the entrance, and escape the company's security location.

The jungle canopy of trees was visually impenetrable. Once they were within it, they would have been hidden from view. If the guerillas had succeeded in entering this area with the expats, they would have been impossible to find as they moved on to the Sierra Nevada de Santa Martas.

Thirty minutes passed before the Colombian military arrived with one attack helicopter, two rubber-tired tanks, and twenty Colombian troops. All thirty of expats were still in the safe room. The guerillas had not found them. They could hear multiple gunshots outside the room from what they thought were the automatic weapons of the onsite security personnel engaging the guerillas. They believed the military's presence would drive the guerillas from the site and would secure the area. However, the expats dared not exit the safe room, as silence was no guarantee that all was clear.

Someone from security finally contacted the group and told them the guerillas had left. They cautiously opened the door to find the military, with weapons drawn, but no guerillas in sight. The group was told the guerillas had escaped into the jungle and that a platoon from the military was chasing them.

They conducted a head-count of all personnel and determined that everyone was accounted for. Two guerillas were dead. Peace returned to the port and work resumed as normal, with the understanding that future attacks were a given.

The problem that they had encountered with the single-engine Cessna, which had caused them to usethe speedier King Air, had led to their early arrival by fifteen minutes of the original schedule. Therefore, they missed the guerillas' planned roadblock at the single-lane bridge and avoided the kidnap of the company's president. This confirmed Arguille's belief in divine intervention.

Aussie Cruise Lines

ARGUILLE WAS INVOLVED with a mining project in the small town of Witbank, South Africa. He befriended an Australian gentleman named Allan. Allan was an electrical engineer who was employed in a contract position in the same project. Arguille introduced himself as Arguille MacGregor, and the two began a get-to-know-each-other conversation. Allan was a vibrant fellow and taught Arguille what it meant to be an Australian mate. Mate status transcends friendship in sincerity and commitment. In time, Arguille attained this status with Allan. There was a three-month rite of passage before he was allowed to achieve the elevated status.

He also instructed Arguille on the three Aussie definitions of the word *bastard*. In each of the definitions, the word was spoken differently: in a monotone, a positive ascending tone, or a negative declining tone. When the word was spoken with a declining tone, it indicated a combative gesture. When it was spoken in monotone, it meant a friendly salutation. When it was spoken with an ascending tone, it indicated a jovial statement and was usually accompanied with the sharing of a pint of dark stout.

Six months into the project, Allan mentioned that a friend was planning to take a two-week vacation and sail from Auckland, New Zealand, to Bora Bora and back. Allan's friend, Michael, who lived in Christ Church, knew of a vessel that was available for rent.

He also knew of a captain he could hire, who would round out his crew with Arguille as a member. The group now had a full crew but was short on experience. They hoped that this problem would be made minimal due to the fact that Captain Ron and Allan were experienced and could train the rest of them in short order.

Captain Ron possessed impeccable credentials and was well qualified to lead us. He had trained for two years in the US and had had eight years of experience in the Pacific, including the Society Islands. The group planned to leave on its journey two weeks later, which was aggressive but doable.

Two weeks later, they all met in Auckland to acquire their vessel and become acquainted. Allan and Arguille traveled from Johannesburg. Their travels were safe and on schedule. They all introduced themselves and sat down in a local pub. They planned to leave two days later, once they had confirmed their sailing route and had rented and inspected their vessel.

The vessel was a forty-eight-foot cutter with a center cockpit, a single mast, diesel-engine backup, and the name *Shillelagh* (This an Irish wooden club that is used to maintain law and order). As the helm would need to be manned twenty-four hours a day, they decided to pair up. The piloting crews were Allan with Arguille and Captain Ron with Michael.

With everyone on board and excited about the journey ahead of them, they maneuvered themselves out of Auckland Harbour (Waitemata Harbour) for Bora Bora. They were all on deck when Captain Ron gave instructions about setting and lowering the sails. The group members' first two attempts showed they were novices, but they became more proficient with additional practice. Once Captain Ron was satisfied group members could handle their tasks, they stood down from the practice exercises.

They set sail and prepared their first meal of the voyage. They were famished from all the activity of the day. Captain Ron was an accomplished chef. He prepared a dinner of steamed fresh prawns, mussels, asparagus, and lettuce wedges. With their hunger satisfied, they all pitched in to clean up and then went topside. The cool mist of the ocean was invigorating, and the potential of spotting sperm whales gave them additional excitement.

They all settled in for the voyage at hand. Captain Ron and Michael would take the first watch until midnight, at which time, Allan and Arguille would take the next watch. On the first night, there were no clouds. The star show was fantastic. In two days, the weather was supposed to change, so they enjoyed the show while conditions allowed. The ocean swells were at five feet, which made the voyage comfortable. No one became seasick. The sleeping accommodations consisted of suspended hammocks, which were below inside the vessel's cabin. Although they did not look very substantial, they were comfortable.

On the second night, the weather began to change. It rained all night, and there was dense fog. Because of these conditions, Allan and Arguille navigated in limited visibility. They could only see two hundred yards ahead, which was not adequate for a rapid response to an emergency. Audible alarms were more reliable than sight, so they used them. However, the distant sound of whales was the only thing they could hear ahead of them at that moment.

Audible alarms for these kinds of maritime conditions were one long blast of our horn and then two short blasts every five minutes, which they initiated at midnight per Captain Ron's instructions. The alarm of an oncoming powered vessel would be one long blast every five minutes but of a distinctly different tone than ours. At this time, the only audible thing in the empty darkness was our own alarm and the sound of the whales. The protocol for night navigation was each sailor to be tethered to the sailboat in the event of rough seas or an emergency.

At approximately 2:30 a.m., Allan and Arguille could hear an alarm from a powered vessel in the north eastern distance. Captain Ron and Michael were oblivious to this as they were in the closed cabin. The alarm was coming ever closer from the northeast, which was the general direction they were traveling. At first, the alarm was faint, but in time, the volume steadily increased. The fog seemed to thicken with the approaching proximity of the vessel. They heard the noise from the wake of the approaching vessel but could not see it.

The oncoming vessel sounded on top of them. Teetering on panic, Arguille decided to go below to wake the captain. As soon as he started for the cabin, Arguille exclaimed, "Oh my God!" Two enormous lights appeared directly in front of the sailboat along with an alarm that was now deafening. Arguille immediately steered the *Shillelagh* hard to starboard, hoping to avoid the huge vessel. The ship turned out to be a liquid petroleum transport that was over six hundred feet in length.

They could not avoid the wake from the huge transport because of the short distance in which they had to maneuver. They were drawn toward the transport, and then the cutter rolled over completely from the huge wake. Somehow, it was uprighted in the same motion. In the process, their single mast was shattered. They all watched as the transport sailed away out of sight. The captain and Michael came up from the cabin. The captain had injured his ribs and broken his arm. Michael was uninjured. The nearest port the group could put into for a hospital and a new mast was Darwin, so they headed in that direction under diesel-engine power at a much reduced speed. Our modified journey took two days with the captain in constant pain.

They harbored in Darwin and immediately took the captain to the hospital. His injuries required a one-week stay for surgery and observation. Michael left us to find a repair shop that could replace our mast.

Being typical Aussies, Allan and Michael located a pub near the boat repair shop. They invited Arguille to join them and began quenching their thirst with their favorite brew of dark stout. This continued for three days. Because of the cost to have the mast repaired, the crew was running low on money. Allan, Michael, and Arguille decided to leave Darwin and sail back to Auckland as their adventure was sadly over. The captain would have to find his own way back once he was released from the hospital. The townspeople of Darwin felt no remorse at seeing the rowdy remaining group members depart.

THE PINK FLAMINGO

ARGUILLE HAD THE good fortune to have been employed on the Colombian Atlantic coast. He was working at a port loading facility near Santa Marta, Colombia. It was a 24-7 operation, which loaded one-hundred-thousand-ton vessels for transport to Asia and Europe.

The material was produced in an area near the Colombian state of Cesar. It was then transported 120 kilometers (75 miles) by train in one-hundred-ton gondolas to the port at Santa Marta. Each unit train carried seventy-five hoppers per transport. Upon arriving at the port, the hoppers were placed in a rotary discharge two at a time. The material was discharged and placed in storage until the next client's ocean cargo vessel arrived for loading. The material was then reclaimed and conveyed to export vessels. The export destinations of the material were mainly Europe and South Korea.

The port area was tropical with a jungle of palm, coconut trees and wild roses. The area was home to poisonous snakes, multiple exotic birds, killer bees, and iguanas. The area also provided a freshwater aquifer supply to the local town of Santa Marta.

Frank, who was a man from Michigan had been an expert in the management of railroads, was assigned to the port's and mine's rail operations as their manager. He and Arguille became friends over time and developed a lasting relationship.

The Colombian government had declared the port area as a refuge for tropical birds and animals. You could not disturb it in any way unless the government approved it in advance.

One day, Arguille's friend Frank and he were driving toward the port's ocean vessel loading station. They passed the protected tropical area. They were looking at it when Frank mentioned that they should plant a pink, plastic lawn flamingo (similar to those found in the southeastern United States) in the area. Arguille thought this would be very funny. He mentioned to Frank that he had a friend who could bring them one within a couple of weeks. Frank said that if he could arrange it, he would help with the task.

As they traveled on to the loading station, the more they thought of the pink flamingo, the more they liked the idea. In two weeks time, Arguille's friend brought a plastic brilliant pink flamingo to the site.

Frank picked a time late at night to plant the flamingo in the protected area. It would be a time when few people were around to observe the deed. The two perpetrators agreed to a midnight plan of action.

Midnight came, and Arguille loaded the brilliant plastic bird into the pickup truck so that they could transport it to the environmental area. Once they were there, Frank retrieved the bird from the pickup and proceeded to the middle of the environmental area. Then Frank planted the bird in the middle of a lush green grassy area. They left and returned to the expatriate compound with their four feet tall artificial bird keeping guard.

The next day, they traveled back to the area where they had planted the bird. From the road, the brilliant pink-colored bird stood out against the jungle green grassy backdrop. Frank and Arguille assumed there would be many questions about the new resident in the protected area. Much to their surprise, the Colombian workers were silent about the new resident and didn't ask any questions. This went on for two weeks. This puzzled Frank and Arguille. Not one worker or staff member said anything.

He and Frank were having lunch at the port's expatriate dining hall. The port's Brazilian manager entered the room, looked at Arguille, and told him that a tour group from the Colombian environmental agency would be arriving soon. The director for the agency would also be in this group of twelve visitors. Arguille replied that he knew of no issues and that the environmental areas were all in good shape.

Once the environmental visitors arrived, they were loaded on the bus and escorted around the site. As they traveled past the environmental area, the Colombian director exclaimed, "Stop the bus! Stop the bus!" He had spotted the pink flamingo. The bus driver stopped the bus abruptly.

They watched for several minutes. Of course, the flamingo did not move. The Colombian director stated that the flamingo must have been tired from traveling and that was the reason the animal had not moved.

The director from the group turned to a Colombian engineer who was traveling with them. Not wanting to frighten the bird the director told the engineer to return later and to get a picture of the flamingo to document its existence. After returning the director then told the port manager that he had instructed the engineer to return for photographs to include the flamingo they had obsereved.

Later, the port manager told me that the environmental director was going to send a group of ten engineers and journalists to camp out at the environmental area. This extended camping in an effort to observe any migration of additional flamingos. He revealed to me that the pink flamingo had been indigenous to Colombia but had left due to pollution. Frank and Arguille had no previous knowledge of the flamingo being indigenous to Colombia. This light hearted prank was approaching a catastrophe.

The director prepared to return to Bogota. He stopped by the administrative office to bid the port manager farewell and to thank him for the tour. The director also stated that he planned to send a group of environmentalists to camp out and to document the flamingos return to the country.

After the environmental group finished their tour and returned to Bogota, the port engineer prepared to take a close-up picture of the flamingo, not knowing it was plastic. He went to his office and retrieved his camera. As he approached the flamingo, it did not fly away. He advanced slowly and got closer and closer, but the flamingo never attempted to fly away. The engineer then became suspicious. He touched the flamingo only to find that it was plastic. He murmured an explicative to himself upon realizing that the flamingo was a fake and the potential for a political and business disaster was in progress. However, he told no one.

One week later, the port engineer received an e-mail from the Colombian environmental director. In that e-mail was a note from the director and a draft copy of an article covering the story of the pink flamingos' return to Colombia. In the e-mail, the director requested that the port engineer review the article and confirm its accuracy. The article was then going to be placed in a Colombian national newspaper named *El Tiempo*, which was circulated nationwide.

The engineer panicked. He went to the port manager and relayed the situation. He then asked the port manager what should be done. If the article was published in Colombia and people learned that it was fake, it would be an embarrassment to the government, stockholders, the parent company, and port management. The collective employment of Frank and Arguille being terminated was a given.

The port engineer wrestled to solve the situation at hand. He decided to contact an environmental engineer in Colombia. The port engineer told the environmental engineer that it was a plastic flamingo, which had been placed there as a decoy to hopefully attract other flamingos back to Colombia. They cancelled the publication of the article. They all breathed a sigh of relief. Frank and Arguille still had employment.

FEMALES OF SOUTH AMERICA

THE FIRST TIME Arguille traveled to South America, he focused his activities on Brazil. As he was looking for adventure, this seemed like the most viable place to achieve that goal. It was a country consisting of iguanas, mosquitoes, cactus, sand, emerald green ocean, guerillas, and beautiful women. Elevations in South America varied from two thousand meters (five thousand feet) in Bogota to sea level in Rio. The combination of these factors gave rise to the potential for an interesting retreat.

Arguille had arrived in Rio at midday. The moisture along with the lack of a breeze and the heat were overwhelming. After deplaning, all passengers entered the un-air-conditioned immigration area in single file.

Brazil had strict regulations on technical equipment and had a habit of confiscating non-compliant equipment. Arguille's sister had packed a spare laptop in his luggage, which he was not aware of. Brazilian regulations allowed one PC per person. Arguille had brought a lap top that he carried thus putting over the limit by one. During his customs inspection, Arguille opened his suitcase as instructed, the illegal, extra laptop fell out. Arguille was shocked. Assuming he was in customs trouble, he lamented under his breath in front of the customs agent, "Oh, *mi hermana*" (my sister).

The agent rapidly questioned, "Does this belong to your sister?"

Arguille hurriedly answered, "Yes."

The agent said, "Okay," and allowed him to pass through customs with the additional computer and to proceed on his_way. Arguille proceeded on to Los Americas Hotel, which was a five-star oceanfront facility. Having traveled from Salt Lake, he was weary and famished from his eighteen hour trip. After check-in, he made his way to the beach side restaurant for a meal and alcohol that he mentioned earlier. After a meal of lobster, a bottle of merlot, and two shots of *aguardiente*, he crashed in his queen-size bed. He had no problem going to sleep.

The next morning, Arguille awoke at 10:30 and proceeded to the hotel's continental buffet. After breakfast, he decided to try out the hotel pool, as the Brazilian midday sun was about to make for an extremely hot day.

Arguille had been sunbathing with his eyes closed beside the pool for an hour when a shadow passed in front of him, prompting him to open his eyes. It turned out to be more than he had imagined it would be. A stunning resembling Latino female, who had a striking resemblance to Sophia Loren, had just walked in front of him. She was approximately six feet tall. Her waist was what looked to be twenty-eight inches, and her bust approached forty-two inches (DD). She walked with an air of grace, determination and confidence.

Needless to say, his attention was aroused. His entire life, he had envisioned that a beautiful woman of color was in his future.

Arguille presumed that she was Brazilian. She was a definite showstopper. All eyes followed her as she strolled around the edge of the pool.

She was in her late thirties and medium build except for the ample bust. She was a brunette with an olive complexion. Her legs were similar to those of a Las Vegas dancer's.

In his adult years on earth, he had a mental vision of meeting a mysterious and beautiful South American woman. He had just found her.

Arguille waited about twenty minutes after his lady of color had gotten comfortable in her poolside chair and then walked over to ask in broken Spanish if he could buy her a margarita. She smiled and accepted his offer, so he joined her. She was currently alone and had come to Rio for a short vacation from her work in Bogota. She was in town for two more days. Her boyfriend had flown back already.

They talked for another hour, and then he invited her to join him for dinner. He asked her for a good restaurant recommendation. She recommended Senor Bebias (Mr. Crocodile) for their dinner. Since Arguille was new to the area, he agreed. The restaurant was located midtown and had outdoor seating and indoor, air-conditioned seating. It was 7:00 p.m., and the dining rooms were only slightly filled with people.

Brazilian culture is not to arrive for dinner until after 9:00 p.m. This is so to people will start dancing versus consuming food, which comes later in the evening. The dining tables are constructed substantially and are firmly anchored to the floor. The females of the country enjoy dancing on top of the tables, which makes for an interesting view.

They enjoyed the fresh seafood dinner and martinis and then joined in the dancing. Brazilian dancing is extremely provocative and hopefully a premonition of future events for Arguille. They danced until 1:00 a.m. and then decided to purchase a ride on a *chiva* bus.

The *chiva* bus is a converted school bus exclusive for dancing, singing, and drinking. It was first used in Colombia and Rio. The driver travels the city, stopping at occasional secure establishments to allow people to continue dancing and partying. We arrived back at the hotel with plenty of *aguardiente* in our system and blurry enthusiasm. Gloria invited Arguille to her room, which initiated anticipation and excitement for the potential end to our evening.

They entered her room. She offered him a tequila and then excused herself for a restroom visit. Arguille drank his tequila while waiting for her return. She returned, and much to his pleasant astonishment, she had wrapped herself in a revealing hotel robe, which was half-open in the front.

Arguille said, "I like your single-access attire."

She replied, "You cannot access my attire from over there."

He did not hesitate but immediately grasped her in his arms began kissing her. He made a point of rubbing his tongue around her lips. I had learned that most women enjoyed this in addition to the standard French protocol. They stood kissing for several minutes.

Then Arguille reached for the single tie on her robe, pulled it with trembling hands, and watched it fall to the floor. As her silhouette had hinted, she was a beautiful woman. He kissed her neck and continued to move down her body. The first time he kissed her ample breasts, she almost collapsed to the floor in ecstasy. This gave him the impression that she had not had her breasts kissed very often and that this was not a habit of Brazilian men.

He continued to give her ecstasy, which instantaneously led to passionate lovemaking. She would sob every time she reached an orgasm—for the next three hours. They fell asleep from their strenuous ecstasy and awoke at noon.

Arguille had spent the night with the most beautiful woman that he had ever met. As time went on, she became his wife.

A Brazilian Bank Robbery

ONE OF THE South American countries Arguille enjoyed visiting while on his adventures was Brazil. Dr. Guzman, who was a college friend and a civil engineer, had invited him to travel to his home country of Brazil. Arguille had not seen Dr. Guzman for two years. He thought that this would be a pleasant visit because Dr. Guzman was an elderly man of great intelligence. His home was located in Rio De Janerio, Brazil, where he had an apartment near the beach.

Arguille checked his calendar and found that he had two week's free for the visit. He told Dr. Guzman that he would be happy to visit Brazil and could travel in two weeks' time. He was delighted and said that the dates were fine with him. They would meet at the Sao Paolo on the way to Rio. He also stated that Arguille could stay at his apartment. They would plan a two-week tour of Brazil, which would include stops at Sao Paulo and the capital city of Brasília.

Arguille boarded his plane for Rio in Salt Lake City. He flew business class, which was very comfortable, roomy and amply supplied with Merlot. The constant flow of Merlot from the flight attendant assisted in lubricating a restful trip. He conversed with the person sitting beside him, who was Brazilian. Arguille learned two things in their conversation. First, the São Paulo International Airport was an older facility surrounded by a city that had grown extensively. Second, the runway was not long enough to accommodate new commercial airplanes. Therefore, if a plane did not touch down on the first one thousand feet of the runway, it could not completely stop on the remaining runway and must take off, circle the airport, and try to land a second time.

As we flew over Rio, we were very close to the tops of the city buildings and the landing required a hard left turn of the aircraft. From inside the plane, it seemed as though the tires would touch the buildings' tops below. This and the situation at the airport raised his blood pressure. Arguille's plane did land within the first one thousand feet of the runway, but it was obvious that the pilot applied full-reverse thrust along with brakes to bring the airplane to a halt. The pilot was successful in landing and bringing the plane to a stop, which we were very grateful for.

Because his career included construction and mining, Dr. Guzman decided to take him to the world's largest iron-ore mine near Paruapebas, Brazil. They were to travel on parallel paths to Belo Horizonte where they would meet. From there, they would continue on to their final destination.

The ore mine was the world's largest mine. The story was told that US Steel Corporation sent four engineers to explore the virgin forest area for iron-ore deposits. Having received no communication for weeks from the engineers, a security force was sent to search the area. After several weeks of investigation, four shrunken heads were recovered. They were identified as belonging to the engineers. The US sent no further personnel to the area. At that time, the indigenous Indians were notorious for this practice.

Arguille was looking forward to the adventure. They were told the area's safety was still equivalent to that of the old Wild West's.

The flight from Belohorizonti to Parauapebas in a twin-engine Otter was uneventful. They traveled in an old taxi for the thirty-minute drive to the mine main office. As they entered the main gate, they were told the mining operations had removed fifteen vertical meters of earth during their first excavation, which had revealed an area of ore that was massive. The exposed ore area was so thick that it had to be excavated in twenty-meter layers to remove the 150 vertical meters of ore. The area would sustain production for four hundred years at current production rates. This was an awesome operation in scale and potential. It was located in the middle of the Amazon Jungle in a fifty-square-mile protected area.

They toured the iron-ore mine and processing infrastructure for most of the morning. The operation included a town with housing for its workers and families. The town was complete with houses, a clinic, a town center, shops, restaurants, and a world-class zoo.

At lunchtime, they left with the provided tour guide, who took them to the main restaurant in the mine town. His name was Jorge, and he was a Brazilian engineer. The restaurant was an outdoor charcoal-grill restaurant in the center of town. With multiple cattle farms nearby, the menu offered ample quality beef. They ordered fillets. The standard entrée included fries, salad, and vegetable items.

The restaurant where they dined was situated in the middle of the business district. Two Banco Brazil banks, a clothing store, and two jewelry stores were near the restaurant. The banks and the jewelry stores were on the far side of the street from Arguille, Dr. Guzman, and the engineer.

As they waited for their order, two police cars pulled up to the banks. One police car parked at one bank, and the second car parked at the other one. Two men each exited the cars in police uniforms caring shotguns and automatic weapons. Because they were dressed in police uniforms and had shotguns, no one gave any thought to the authenticity of the situation. Arguille observed two men enter each bank. They then heard a crackling noise. Their first thought was that it was nearby fireworks. The trio then saw people running away from the bank past their location indicating the crackling noise was gun shots.

They realized they were in the middle of two robberies. The robbers must have entered each bank and demanded all available cash to be handed over to them. A bank official had later recanted that one robber had demanded that a customer give him all the cash he had. The customer responded that it was his personal money. The robber told the customer to keep the money and that he only wanted money from the bank.

After all the cash was retrieved from each bank, the robbers took each manager and one clerk as their hostages. After they exited the banks, they smashed the windows of the adjacent jewelry stores and removed all the jewelry.

At the sound of the first gunshots, everyone in the restaurant scrambled to exit through the back of the building. Dr. Guzman crawled under our table, jumped a nearby hedge, and ran away with the rest of the locals. Arguille did not realize a man of Dr. Guzman's age could run that fast.

They were told that the robbers were taking expatriates as hostages also. Local schools and business offices were behind the restaurant and vacant. The trio entered one of the school's classrooms, locked the door, and listened in silence for evidence of movement. The only thing they could hear were their hearts pounding in fear. They were there for thirty minutes with no audible indication that others were in the building. They cautiously peered out of the room. No one was close by. They then left the building, walked to the restaurant, and found that the robbers had left.

That afternoon, they learned from authorities that the robbers had a prearranged meeting location in the jungle where an escape helicopter would be waiting. On further investigation, Arguille learned that the robbers had left the area in two cars. Three hundred yards from the restaurant, the robbers had stopped, turned one car ninety degrees to block the highway, and had set the car on fire, which blocked traffic. They had then driven into the jungle, rendezvoused with an awaiting helicopter, and escaped. At the rendezvous, they had released the hostages and disappeared into the Amazon sky.

Tiananmen Square

IN 1987, ARGUILLE completed his college undergraduate studies and decided to obtain employment overseas. His major had been in engineering, but he always had a desire to go into construction.

He ran into Larry, who was a friend working in China's mining industry, which was expanding rapidly and had construction project jobs in operations, commercial, and infrastructure. Larry told him that the company was looking for young engineers to work in these projects. This sounded interesting to Arguille because he had never worked outside of his birth country before and found this enticing.

Larry arranged an interview for Arguille with the American company. In the interview, he was told that the company was looking for engineers who were single, no children, and wanted overseas experience in construction. The project was funded by a large oil company and the Chinese government. The project would cost approximately $1 billion. Even though he lacked field experience, his credentials were what the company was looking for. They explained his pay, housing, and other benefits.

The salary was 20 percent higher than the same position in the US. Couple this with a 28 percent increase in pay for the expatriate-income-tax deduction, and it created a lucrative package. They would also pay Arguille a 15 percent completion bonus at the end of 36 months. Several housing options were available: three apartment buildings for singles, several condos for married couples, and thirty-five houses of Chinese construction and Spanish design for future families. Medical support was provided by a Canadian physician and one registered nurse.

The work schedule was six weeks working on-site and one week for R&R. Transportation to the site by rail from Beijing took fifteen hours to complete, with a two-hour layover in Datong. An additional benefit was an annual four-week vacation that included a mandatory physical.

During the next part of the interview, Arguille would speak with the project director. He entered the director's office and noticed that three chairs were facing the director's desk. One chair was on the far left side, one chair was on the far right side, and one chair was directly in front of the director. Arguille perceived this was a test of tenacity, so he sat in the chair that was directly in front of the director.

The director introduced himself as Fred Shorty. Arguille introduced himself, and they started their professional conversation. The director commented that Arguille's background and family history helped meet the position requirements. The director said that he had already checked his background. He had spoken to the people who were on his professional recommendation list and who were already working on the project. He was in a position to offer Arguille employment. The offer was substantial, so that and the thought of an overseas adventure were enough to cause Arguille to accept the position.

Because he already possessed a passport and a Chinese visa and had had a physical and background check, he was able to leave for China. Arguille arrived in Beijing at ten o'clock at night and entered the one-terminal airport. Arguille cleared immigration and went into the lobby. No one was there to receive him, so he looked around the taxi area.

Then he noticed one Chinese driver in the middle of the crowd holding a sign that read, "MacGregor." I went to the individual and quickly learned he spoke no English. Because his face looked honest, Arguille followed the driver to his car, and they exited the airport.

As they drove toward the downtown area, Arguille noticed there were no streetlights. It was extremely dark, and as they proceeded, a vehicle approached them from the opposite direction. The vehicle was approximately two hundred yards away from them. As they approached the vehicle, its driver turned off his headlights. All of the oncoming-traffic drivers did the same.

It was the Chinese custom for oncoming-traffic drivers to turn their lights off at night so they would not offend other drivers. Arguille was silent and imagined trying to drive in the dark with oncoming vehicles with no lights. This was his first indication he would have a bona fide adventure in China.

Arguille stayed at a hotel in Beijing that night. Early the next day, he left for the train station. As it was the middle of the winter, many peasants had moved into the train station along with their farm animals for warmth. The driver had gone there to obtain my ticket for the fifteen-hour journey that he would take to the site.

The site was near a town named Xiaoxiang. It was a thriving town, which was located near the place where Mao Tse-tung had started his long march that had brought him to power. The area was arid with little or no grass or trees. It was just south of the Gobi Desert.

Previously, Chairman Mao had removed all the trees to eliminate birds from feeding in the fields. This of course led to insect pestilence, which could not be controlled for many years. The only trees that existed had been manually planted over the last fifteen years. They were in rows along the roadways.

Arguille noticed some fire towers that were twenty feet by twenty feet at their bases and sixty feet high clay structures. These towers had been illuminated when the Mongolians from the north had attacked the local towns. Fires would be ignited on top of these towers to signal a warning of invasion to the inhabitants of the south.

The living quarters were in the center of town. The three apartment buildings for Chinese suppliers, the condos for married couples, a hotel, and the thirty-five Spanish-designed houses for families encircled this area. I learned the different cultures that included personnel from Hungary, Canada, the United States, England, Germany, Australia, and Jamaica. The hotel kitchen served both Chinese and European cuisine. The hotel had fifteen floors. The restaurant was on the first floor, and the bar, which closed at ten o'clock, was on the second floor.

During his first night at the hotel, Arguille was not familiar with the Australian custom and propensity for beer consumption. Because of this, he made the mistake of going to the bar after dinner. There were six Aussies throwing darts, which is a common Australian pass time. They were enjoying themselves. The atmosphere was thick with conversations. At ten o'clock, the Chinese bartender officially closed the second floor bar. The Aussies supplied two cases of Tsingtao beer to unofficially reopen the bar. The conversations and the dart contest continued until 2 a.m. In typical Chinese fashion, all outside doors were padlocked or chained, making returns to our living areas difficult.

Early the next morning after breakfast, Arguille was escorted to the operations site. Along the twenty-mile highway, he saw approximately two hundred Chinese boys from the ages of fifteen to seventeen manually widening the highway with picks and shovels. There were no bulldozers or loaders. The use of manual labor had been mandated due to a 1.5 billion population. These youths labored from sunrise until sunset every day. They widened the highway by twenty feet horizontally and twenty feet vertically for fifteen miles. All the materials movement was to be accomplished by hand.

The travelers were provided with their own transportation, which required passing a Chinese driving test. This test consisted of an actual driving test with two Chinese police officers in the test vehicle to observe their driving-skill expertise. On the day of the test, a Canadian engineer, who was fluent in Mandarin Chinese, was to accompany them during the test drive.

On the day of the test, the Canadian engineer joined Arguille for breakfast at 8:00 at the site's hotel. The engineer's name was Richard. After introductions were made, they both sat down for breakfast.

Richard had many opportunities to travel with expats who were getting their licenses and was familiar with the Chinese officers who conducted the test. Richard informed Arguille that none of the officers spoke or understood English.

That being the case, Richard informed Arguille that when the officers would ask a question, he would ask Arguille the question in English. The question would not necessarily be the same in content as the Chinese version. Richard informed Arguille that he could respond on any subject incorrectlybut he would translate the correct answer to the officers. After driving the test vehicle and answering twenty questions incorrectly, I passed my test with the aide of the Canadian translator.

During this period, China was experiencing a major economic boom after President Nixon's success at opening the country to the US economic development. All areas of infrastructure and economy had been stagnant prior to this event and under the leadership of Mao Tse-tung. After his passing and the rise of Teng Hsiao-p'ing to power, there was a massive effort to bring China's economy forward. Alongside this effort, there was one to develop a democratic society in place of the established communist government.

College-aged students began a civil protest in Tiananmen Square to draw attention to their cause for democracy-related issues. They included a six-foot-tall Statue of Liberty to further express their cause in the square. Protests continued throughout the country with violent uprisings at some locations. About 150,000 protesters had accumulated in Tiananmen Square in Beijing.

During this time, Russia was planning a state visit to China with Mikhail Gorbachev leading the entourage. Meetings were planned in Beijing along with tours of local cultural facilities for the international state visitors. Russian visitors felt that the Tiananmen Square protest had grown to the point that every area of the country had been affected. They found the streets of Beijing choked with Chinese students and the general population, which were assembling at or near the square. This scenario created a security liability that forced the visiting dignitaries to reconsider their security preparedness and to return to Moscow. This was a direct insult to the Beijing government, which caused it and its people to *lose face*.

The Chinese government could not let this internationally visible event continue. The Russian officials' retreat to their own country due to the volatility of the political situation would potentially escalate into civil war. Internal decisions were made to use the Chinese military's intervention to clear the situation in the square. The decision to use military force was agreed upon, was approved by Teng Hsiao-p'ing, and was executed on June 4.

On this day, Arguille was staying in the Lido Hotel. When he arrived, he was astonished to observe a military truck stationed outside the hotel with armed Chinese troops in the back waiting for the order to clear the square.

The military began clearing the square at 7:30 p.m. on June 4. Earlier that day, two of Arguille's companions had gone to the square to observe the situation and to photograph the activities. Arguille received a call from them at around 8:30 p.m. He could hear screaming and gunfire in the background.

One of his friends said, "Arguille, do not come to Tiananmen Square, as people are being shot by the military."

Arguille noticed military trucks headed in the opposite direction of the square and questioned a taxi driver about where they were going. He said that they were carrying dead bodies from the square to a *crematorium* to minimize the body count from the military's attack on the square.

The military procession of trucks carrying the deceased continued the entire night, which indicated that there was a large amount of bodies to transport. Armed military personnel marched up and down the hotel hallways maintaining security.

Of course, they were nervous and stressed. Their mates told him about their trip to the square, which did not reduce Arguille's anxiety level when he learned of the violence that they had encountered. This was further compounded by what they learned from hotel management: The airport in Beijing had been closed to commercial traffic.

The group collectively decided that they wanted to return to the US as soon as possible because the situation in China seemed to be heading toward civil war. They began their attempt to contact the American embassy at 5 a.m. but did not get through until 8:00 a.m. They were instructed to be at the airport by 2:00 p.m., as there were two 737s that were leaving for Los Angeles carrying US citizens only. No other flights were scheduled. They gave them their information and were confirmed for seats on the plane.

The group left the hotel at 11:00 a.m., which turned out to be good planning. The roads to the airport were jammed with civilians protesting. It was estimated that over one million Chinese had joined the melee. They made their way to the air-freight terminal after passing through customs and an armed security area. Their passports were checked for the fourth time, and they were allowed to board.

There was a sense of relief when they boarded. It felt as if they were safe. The plane was fully loaded. Conversations among the passengers were extremely limited because passengers were stressed due to the situation.

Two hours later, we were in the air and going in an easterly direction. We all cheered when the wheels up (takeoff) took place. *God bless the USA!*

URICH

LOUIS, AN ASSOCIATE of Arguille's, approached him concerning an adventure trip to Poland. He said that he had friends there and that he was going for a one-week trip. Having never been to the country and having some idle time on his hands, he accepted the offer. Two weeks later, they found themselves on a LOT Polish Airlines flight to Warsaw. LOT was a relatively new airline company owned and operated by Polish businessmen. We made the flight in six hours because we had a favorable tailwind assisting the plane versus its usual eight-hour flight time.

Warsaw's buildings looked relatively new. Arguille questioned his friend about this because Arguille thought it was an older city. His response was that the original city had been leveled by the Germans during World War II and had later been reconstructed.

After clearing customs, his Polish friend Urzy met them. He was a friendly fellow and spoke excellent English. He was of medium build and smoked cigarettes continuously. He introduced himself and then directed them to an awaiting taxi. They arrived at the Continental Hotel, which was a five-star facility. The hotel was situated in a picturesque square that encompassed the Polish Tomb of the Unknown Soldier. This tomb was guarded twenty-four hours a day by the military.

Urzy had planned a day for us in Krakow, which had been Poland's capital until the 1600s when it had been moved to Warsaw. Krakow was protected by the United Nations. Any construction, including repairs to the cobblestoned streets, had to have UN approval. Not only were the city sights available but a nearby salt mine in Valencia was also in close proximity to Krakow.

The salt mine had three levels and had been in operation for three hundred years. Salt was the only means of preserving food during this time before refrigeration. The mine also served in many other capacities: as a fighter-plane-engine-assembly floor for the Nazi's, a place for overnight stays for asthma sufferers, and a dance venue with restaurant.

Massive carvings had been done along the walls of an excavation site by two brothers, which depicted the life of Jesus Christ: his birth, the "Sermon on the Mount," Palm Sunday, the Last Supper, the Crucifixion, and many other life-sized events in the life of Christ. A six-foot-tall salt statue of the Virgin Mary had been etched in a room, which also had a massive salt chandelier suspended from the ceiling for lighting. In our journey, this place alone made our trip a worthwhile adventure.

It was late afternoon, so they left Valencia and traveled to Katowice, Urzy's hometown. Urzy's wife had prepared dinner for them, which they had not expected. As they walked through the door, the aroma from her food preparation was awesome. This activated their stomachs' digestive juices immediately. They were introduced to Urzy's wife, Eva, who was a beautiful woman of medium height. She had brilliant blue eyes, long blond hair, and stunning overall looks. Her English was broken but understandable.

The apartment was typical of those constructed in the Soviet Union days. They were made of solid concrete and had no individuality. To reduce the cost of the construction, there wasn't access to the elevator on every floor. Odd numbered apartments were accessible on the first floor, and even numbered apartments were accessible on the next and staggered the entire building elevation.

There was a splendid setting of appetizers, which was fit for royalty. After Arguille and Richard had done their best to sample all the appetizers and had gotten acquainted with Eva, they were introduced to Urzy's specialty meal—*czarn kaczka* (black duck). He brought the entrée on a tabletop electric grill and placed it on the dining room table in front of them.

The site and aroma from the grilled fowl put their digestive juices into overdrive. Urzy immediately began carving the huge fowl and serving each of the guests. As he served it, Urzy told them that the meat had to be consumed while it was still hot. Even if they were already full, they had to devour the entire duck. We finished the delicious fowl and lubricated it with the better portion of a bottle of Polish vodka.

During the dinner, Urzy and Eva related the painful story of their twenty-one-year-old son passing away due to cancer. His passing occurred not long after the Chernobyl nuclear reactor failure. They were downwind of the facility. They attributed his passing to the effects of this event. They had no other children, and this caused a great deal of sadness, which was obvious in their conversational tone.

All the guests ate their fill and thanked Urzy and Eva for their efforts. Urzy presented them with very ornate, twenty-inch daggers, which was a Polish custom. As they were preparing to leave, Urzy told them that they could now call him Urich because we were his friends. We were unaware of this Polish custom. Urich had just given them a great personal honor.

The group returned to their hotel and noticed a small pub nearby. Arguille and Louis decided to stop for a nightcap before returning to their rooms. The pub seemed to attract blue-collar types of workers. Inside, it was not elaborately designed but in a typical Polish way. They had just consumed their third and final Zywiec (Polish beer) when Arguille decided to take a picture of the crew before they departed. The bartender obliged them by taking the picture. He even inadvertently captured other patrons in the background. Once it was completed, Arguille retrieved his camera, and they proceeded to their rooms.

All the food, alchol, and activity of that day caused Arguille to go to sleep early. At 2:30 a.m., he was pulled from a deep sleep. In an instant, he realized that there were two strangers in his room. They began to place tape over his mouth and used the phone cord to tie his hands. They forced Arguille onto the floor. One of the men was going through the drawers and bathroom cabinet. The thug that was holding him on the floor noticed that he was trying to turn his head to see what was taking place. The thug took the dagger that Arguille had left on the nightstand and ran the blade down the back of my head. Arguille could feel the blade as it ground against the strands of his hair and then followed the contour of my skull. Then he drove it through the back of my ear and forced the point into the carpet, which restricted his movement.

When the other thug located his camera, both men talked briefly in Polish. When the man pulled the dagger out of my ear, he feared that his death was imminent. The thug untied Arguille's hands, and both men left the room with camera in hand. As Arguille looked around the room, he saw his blood was on the carpet, bedspread, and the room chairs. The only thing missing from the room was the camera. All of Arguille's credit cards, cash, and his passport were still there. A large bloodstain was also on the floor.

Arguille was in shock but managed to go to Louis's room and wake him. He had Louis take him to the nearest hospital where they stitched up the cuts in his ear. The dagger had narrowly missed the ear drum. When they returned to the hotel room, the room had been scrubbed clean to remove all evidence of the blood-stained attack. There was no need to file a police report as the evidence had been obliterated by hotel management.

The next day, the group learned that two of the people that had been in Arguille's camera pictures were fugitives thus the reason for the attack. Arguille learned a lesson: Never go to an unknown area of a foreign country without speaking the language and without bringing someone who is familiar with the culture with you.

INDONESIA

THE EXPERIENCES ARGUILLE acquired in Indonesia began with an invitation to assist in a problem-solving exercise in a Jepara, Indonesia project. An engineer from Chicago had contacted him concerning the restart of a Japanese construction project that had been idle for six years due to financial issues.

Arguille traveled thirty-two hours by plane from Salt Lake City to Semarang and then two-and-a-half hours by car to Jepara, the site location. This area in Indonesia was noted for its wealth of teakwood. Several Norwegian families had immigrated there to start furniture businesses, so the location around Jepara had many Norwegian inhabitants. They had been very successful at this venture. Several families had become millionaires in the teakwood business.

One in particular was Mr. Fred Sorensen. He had succeeded so well that he had purchased his own island locally and had developed a small resort. The Sorensen family consisted of a mother, a father, three daughters, two brothers, and a grandfather. The grandfather had been the original family member who immigrated to Indonesia along with his extended family at that time. The entire family was tall, blond, blue-eyed, and strikingly well structured. The males were strong, and the females were well proportioned.

The two young males were in their early twenties and were typical of their age and heritage. Marijuana and beer were readily available, and Jorg and Steven were regular consumers. They all had a working knowledge of Johnny Horton songs. Arguille never determined what prompted their love of Johnny Horton music, but he often entered into a rendition of "The Battle of New Orleans" when they were in a musical mood, which happened on a regular basis. This all took place in the only European-style pub in Jepara a town with a population of 15,000.

A favorite pastime of his Norwegian friends was to purchase used Willys Jeeps of the World War II vintage, refurbish them, upgrade them to a monster-type design, and ride through Indonesian jungles and swamps. One such outing included three Norwegian fun seekers and Arguille. They had traveled for two hours through the thick Indonesian vegetation and were ready to return home.

They used the nearest one-and-a-half-lane asphalt highway for their return. As is standard for the area, the road was jammed with motorbikes—the normal mode of transportation for the three hundred million inhabitants. The highway had no standard directions, guardrails, or road markings, and total concentration was required to avoid collisions.

As they entered a sharp right-hand turn at a high rate of speed, oncoming motorized bike appeared in the oncoming lane. Jorg was driving and instinctively turned right to avoid the bike rider. He avoided the bike, but his monster jeep left the road, rolled over in a nearby stream, and landed upside down. If not for the roll bar they had added, they would have all perished instantly.

Steven was trapped under the back seat. He was trapped upside down in the stream. The group attempted to lift the vehicle off

Steven, but all the added weight from the monster upgrade made it impossible to lift. It was horrifying to stand by and helplessly listen to the gasping breaths and screams of a close friend as he was drowning. Steven was twenty-seven years old, the father of a three-month-old baby girl and a wife the day the accident happened.

We commandeered the aid of six Indonesians and manually lifted the Jeep off Steven. It was too late. We administered artificial respiration for an hour but observed no response. This ended Arguille's beer and marijuana days.

Three Walked In, and Four Walked Out

ARGUILLE HAD SPENT the day on the beach in Cartagena. It had been a slow, relaxing day with gentle ocean breezes and multiple vendors walking the beach. The vendors included minstrels with three singers and one scrub board player, a manicurist, a sunglasses and T-shirt vendor, and prostitutes. The songs were all in Spanish and were the same rhythm.

Cold beer was served at a thatched-roof kiosk near the beach. The owners' names were Pollo and Juanita. Pollo was Juanita's husband and had the physique of Emmett Smith, the professional football player.

Arguille had lunch outside at the Bonnie restaurant. This restaurant specialized in freshly caught saltwater pan-fried fish. The server would bring a platter with several species of fresh fish displayed on it. These fish had been cleaned with the heads kept intact. The species included sea bass, red snapper, and wahoo. Each fish was in the five-to-eight-pound range. You chose the fish you wanted, and your selection was immediately taken to the open-air kitchen to be fried.

Once completed, the waiter returned with the cooked entrée, which included potato fries, cooked rice, and salad. Sitting in the ocean breeze with palm trees swaying in the wind was a motivation and an incentive to satisfy your appetite there. They enjoyed our lunch to the last morsel.

They had their fill of cold beer and lunch and returned to their hotel. They agreed to rest for a couple of hours and to meet in the lobby for dinner. The time was useful in getting the sand and lotion off in a soothing shower.

The group met in the lobby at six o'clock. They hailed a taxi, and per the instructions of their host who was also the project manager, they proceeded to the Mr. Babia restaurant. The drive through Cartagena was slow because it was crowded with shoppers, revelers, and vendors. It was a thirty-minute ride to the restaurant.

Because they were expatriates, they had been warned to be cognizant of motorcycles with two riders. As the kidnapping of expatriates was not unusual, motorcycles with two riders could be a problem. One could be the driver, and the other could be a shooter. One of the mine's secretaries had been assassinated the week before, involving this scenario. The secretary had been involved in labor-relations issues and had been assertive with the local labor union. The union had included a guerilla presence, which they were not familiar with.

They arrived at the restaurant close to seven o'clock. They entered the restaurant, and for the most part, it was vacant. The Mr. Babia restaurant had a thatched roof, but the seating was also outside. As this was a seafood restaurant, the aroma of shrimp and lobster permeated the air and accelerated their digestive juices. They located a table in anticipation. After the server took their orders, it was only a short time before it was ready.

As the nine o'clock hour approached, the group noticed that the restaurant was filling with patrons. The host told them the custom was to begin dinner at nine o'clock. Colombian music was playing continuously. It was the custom for female patrons to get on table tops and danced to the music. This lasted until the wee hours of the morning. The noise was tremendous, but the table top view was exciting.

Two engineers in the group decided to go next door to visit another establishment. Arguille said that he would join them later as he had not finished his lobster. Once he had finished the large crustacean, he left to join his friends next door. The only problem was that they did not tell Arguille which direction to turn once he had left the restaurant. Of course with his luck, he turned left, and his friends had turned right.

Arguille turned left and went into the establishment after paying a twenty-dollar cover charge. As he walked into the dance area, he realized that the patrons were all drug-induced zombies attempting to dance. He also realized that it was not the establishment that his friends had gone to. They must have taken a right turn when he took a left.

There was a bar near the exit and parallel to the wall. While in the bar, Arguille decided to have a drink before he left, so he ordered *aguardiente* (better known in English as fire water) at the bar. He finished his drink, and he was getting ready to leave when he noticed the exit doors. Two Colombian military personnel with automatic weapons were now blocking the exit. It was a drug bust.

The first universal truth that Arguille learned in foreign business and travel was to always stay calm no matter what happened and not to panic. If you became excited or unfocused, you stopped thinking. Therefore, he waited patiently at the bar and observed the situation so that he could plot his next move. During this time, Arguille noticed someone exiting the dance floor with a handful of pesos and approaching a military person at the exit.

Arguille realized that this was his opportunity. The bribe was in place. The person went back to the dance floor and approached his two companions. The party of three was walking toward him and the exit. As they approached, Arguille stepped into their party of three. They now were a party of four. They walked to the end of the bar, passed the military personnel, and exited the building unrestricted. Arguille had been sweating bullets as he had walked past the soldiers. He had been very concerned that he would be stopped at the exit, but he had not been.

Arguille returned to Mr. Babia where his two friends had already arrived. Needless to say, he was upset and used many four-letter expletives to express his anger. He had just missed an opportunity to visit a Colombian house of incarceration, which he would not have relished being a *gringo* in Colombia.

All in all, the evening turned out to be a memorable event, which could have turned into a catastrophe. Arguille learned to make sure he was following the crowd to the correct location in future similar situations. They all finished the evening at Mr. Babias and returned safely to the hotel. They individually pondered what their next Colombian adventure would encompass.

Over time, Arguille MacGregor has been presented with many opportunities to travel globally, escape kidnapping attempts, experience many different cultures, establish many international friendships, and meet the love of his life. He often wonders why he has been so blessed in life but can only answer that question with the stories of his continued adventures and what destiny awaits.

www.ingramcontent.com/pod-product-compliance
Lightning Source LLC
Chambersburg PA
CBHW030652190726
48286CB00008B/2777